Chestnut Cove

Written and Illustrated by Tim Egan

Houghton Mifflin Company
Boston

For Christopher and Brian,
my wonderful sons

For information about this and other Houghton Mifflin trade and reference
books and multimedia products, visit The Bookstore at Houghton Mifflin on
the World Wide Web at http://www.hmco.com/trade/.

Library of Congress Cataloging-in-Publication Data

Egan, Tim.
  Chestnut Cove / Tim Egan.
     p. cm.
  Summary: When King Milford offers his entire kingdom to the person
who can grow the largest juiciest watermelon, the inhabitants of
Chestnut Cove become selfish and stop helping each other.
    RNF ISBN 0-395-69823-5   PAP ISBN 0-395-85076-2
    [1. Watermelons–Fiction. 2. Selfishness–Fiction.]   I. Title.
PZ7.E2815Ch   1995   94-17367
[E]–dc20   CIP
                         AC

Manufactured in the United States of America

BVG   10 9 8 7 6 5 4 3 2

$\mathbb{T}$he fog clears at about ten o'clock every morning at Chestnut Cove. As the sun warms the town, the villagers tend to their wonderful gardens, the shopkeepers open their doors, and the children trot off to school.

You can usually find Mrs. Lark strolling along the cliffside with her pig, Eloise. And sometimes you might see the Ferguson family having somersault races in the town square.

Mrs. Ferguson wins most of the time.

Interesting things are always happening in Chestnut Cove. Like when Joe Morgan's cow, Thelma, got stuck way up in an oak tree. It took half the town to get her down.

Everyone's still trying to figure out how she got up there.

Another time, the Fergusons' fish drank up their pond. There was a frantic rush to get him to the lake as quickly as possible. As strange as things may get, everybody always tries to help one another out.

Well, one day late last winter, the town was awakened by the sounds of bells and trumpets. It was the ship of King Milford—a cause for excitement. It was also seven o'clock in the morning, and though some folks didn't seem quite ready to get up, they did anyway.

King Milford was a fine leader, and most everyone liked him.
He wore a top hat instead of a crown and had a rather strange
fondness for watermelons, but he was a fair and decent ruler.

The king lived in a magnificent castle on a nearby island. He had been traveling for three days to each and every village in the land with the same incredible announcement. "Whosoever grows the largest and juiciest watermelon by summer's end shall inherit my entire kingdom. Good luck!" he said.

Then he left.

Everyone laughed at the whole ridiculous idea and went on with the day as usual.

Some folks just went back to bed.

But over the next few days, the villagers started thinking about all the wonderful things they could have if they inherited the king's riches.

Mrs. Phillips imagined all the beautiful dresses and fancy hats she could buy. She just loved fancy hats.

And the Johnsons knew they could build a bigger ranch and have a lot more pets . . . as if they needed more pets.

Joe Morgan could buy the nicest wagon in the land. He was suddenly tired of his old wagon, even though he built it himself.

And Mr. Ferguson could buy his own ship, which he and his family could sail away on. It was endless how much they didn't have.

The following week was quieter than usual. Everyone was busy gardening, turning the soil and planting watermelons.

As the weeks went by and the melons began to grow, the villagers of Chestnut Cove began to change. They didn't talk to

each other as much because they were all so busy. Some of them even built fences around their gardens so that no one could touch their watermelons.

It seemed that Mrs. Lark was growing the largest one. It was bigger than Eloise the pig, yet smaller than Thelma the cow.

Mrs. Lark started sleeping in her garden at night so that nobody could steal her amazing watermelon.

Joe Morgan's watermelon was pretty impressive, too. He stood guard all day with Thelma and would throw a bucket of her milk at anyone who got too close.

Things weren't good.

You could tell everything had changed when, one day, Mrs. Phillips's goat got his horns stuck in the park bench and nobody, not even Mrs. Phillips, was there to help.

By harvest time, things were even worse. Everyone was fighting over who had the best watermelon. The king was coming the next day and they all worked late into the afternoon preparing. The streets were crowded but no one was saying a word.

21

Then, just as the sun was going down, Mrs. Lark came running into the town screaming, "It's Eloise! She's fallen off the cliff! My poor little pig is stuck on a ledge. Please, can't somebody help?"

Well, in a moment the whole town went running toward the cliff. Everyone knew and loved Eloise, and would do anything to save that little pig.

It was a tremendous effort. They brought rope and shovels and hammers and wrenches. Of course, all they needed was the rope, so they put the other stuff down and lowered Joe Morgan along the side of the cliff toward Eloise.

It was scary and great at the same time.

When it was over, about twenty minutes later, Eloise and Joe were safe. Mrs. Lark, her eyes filled with emotion, stood up and said, "Thank you all so much. And, um, nothing against Milford, the watermelon king, but I personally think this whole contest is, well . . . stupid. In fact, I'm going to go home and eat mine before he even sees it. Would anyone care to join me?"

Everyone was quiet for a moment. Then one of the Ferguson kids yelled, "Picnic in the town square!"

Five minutes later, everybody gathered at the square with breads and cheeses and drinks and shovels. Once again, they didn't need the shovels, but someone kept bringing them anyway.

Oh, and they brought watermelons. The most beautiful watermelons that anyone had ever seen.

They danced and ate all night long. When it was over, the
only watermelons that were left were a few rotten-looking ones.

The next morning, as expected, the king showed up. He looked at the watermelons that were left.

He wasn't very impressed.

As he boarded his ship he said, "I'm afraid these are the most disappointing watermelons I've seen yet. They are, quite

frankly, disgraceful. I believe you all need to work on your gardening skills."

And as his ship pulled away, the villagers of Chestnut Cove looked rather sad.

But they weren't sad at all, they were just tired from staying up all night.